THE ENCHANTED TUNNEL

BOOK TWO

ESCAPE FROM EGYPT

THE ENCHANTED TUNNEL

BOOK TWO
ESCAPE FROM EGYPT

Marianne Monson

Illustrated by Dan Burr

DESERET
BOOK

SALT LAKE CITY, UTAH

Library of Congress Cataloging-in-Publication Data
Monson, Marianne.
 Escape from Egypt / Marianne Monson.
  p. cm. — (The enchanted tunnel ; bk. 2)
 Audience: 4-6
 Summary: Twins Nathan and Aria use the tunnel under the stage in their church's cultural hall to travel back to ancient Egypt and witness the exodus of Israel led by Moses.
 ISBN 978-1-60641-670-9 (paperbound)
  1. Time travel—Juvenile fiction. 2. Exodus, The—Juvenile fiction.
3. Egypt—Antiquities—Juvenile fiction. 4. Fantasy fiction, American.
5. Children's stories, American. [1. Space and time—Fiction. 2. Exodus, The—Fiction. 3. Moses (Biblical leader)—Fiction. 4. Mormons—Fiction.
5. Brothers and sisters—Fiction. 6. Twins—Fiction.]
I. Title. II. Series: Monson, Marianne. Enchanted tunnel series ; bk. 2.
 PZ7.M76282Esc 2010
 [Fic]—dc22   2010001321

Printed in the United States of America
Malloy Lithographing Incorporated, Ann Arbor, MI

10 9 8 7 6 5 4 3 2 1

For the real Nathan and Aria, with love

A BIG THANK-YOU

Special thanks to Dr. Jeffrey Chadwick, professor of archaeology and Near Eastern studies at Brigham Young University, for his invaluable knowledge of the history and region, which he so willingly shared with me.

A NOTE TO THE READER

When I read a good book, I like to know if it *really* happened. *The Enchanted Tunnel* books are historical fiction, which means that part is true and part is made up. Nathan and Aria and their adventures in the enchanted tunnel are imagined, but the events from the scriptures are true. They *really* happened.

Some of the details, such as what the characters were eating or doing on a specific day, are invented, but they are the types of things people of the time *often* ate or did. You can read more about the true stories that relate to Nathan and Aria's adventures by looking at the section called "To Learn More" on page 83 at the end of the book.

When I was a child, I sometimes found it difficult to relate to people from scripture stories because they lived so long ago. Thankfully, I had wonderful parents and teachers who brought the scriptures to life. These teachers opened a magic tunnel in my mind and helped me to imagine myself in the scripture stories. It is my hope that the *Enchanted Tunnel* books will do the same for you.

1

A PROPHET LIKE MOSES

Brother King looked down at his lesson manual. "What types of jobs did pioneer children help with?" he asked.

Nathan waved his hand in the air.

Brother King looked surprised. "Nathan?"

"They had to work hard," said Nathan. "The kids found firewood, took care of oxen, and made food."

"And milked cows," added Aria. She smiled at Nathan, her twin brother.

"And sometimes there were mountain storms," said Nathan. "So their clothes got soaking wet and dirty."

Brother King nodded. "You're sure a lot more interested in pioneers than you were last week." He looked curiously from Nathan to Aria.

"We did some research," said Aria.

"I can tell," said Brother King. "One last thing. Brigham Young led thousands of pioneers into the desert to find a new home. Can anyone guess which prophet they compared him to?"

"Noah?" guessed Nathan's friend Ben.

"Nephi?" asked Nathan.

Brother King shook his head.

"Hmmm," said Aria. "Is it Moses?"

"Yes," said Brother King. "Why?"

Aria looked thoughtful. "Probably because Moses led the children of Israel through the desert to the promised land."

"Exactly," said Brother King. "They said the pioneers were just like the Israelites."

Nathan made a face at his friend Ben. Ben

grinned. It was so annoying when Aria knew all the answers.

Nathan reached for his scripture bag. Even though he liked Brother King, he couldn't wait for the lesson to end. He was dying to get back to the tunnel. The *enchanted* tunnel, Aria had started calling it. Would it still work? He had to find out.

A girl named Katie said the closing prayer.

Nathan grabbed his bag and started to leave, but Brother King called him back. "Keep doing research, Nathan," he said. "And maybe you could bring in the book to show the rest of the class."

The twins looked at each other. "Um . . . we could try," said Aria.

Nathan tried really hard not to crack up. He nodded.

"'Bye, Brother King," said Aria.

"'Bye!"

Nathan pulled open the door and waved good-bye to Ben.

Nathan and Aria headed down the hall to look for their mother. "That was so funny!" said Nathan.

"I'm not sure we can really explain our research," agreed Aria.

"Let's go to the tunnel! I'm excited to see Joseph F."

"I hope the tunnel still works," said Aria.

"I think it will," said Nathan. "And I'm prepared this time." He pointed to his scripture bag. "I've got the GPS, lights, water, and snacks."

"Perfect," said Aria. "I brought my tennis shoes. Let's find Mom."

She was in the Relief Society room, talking, of course. She turned. "I have to talk to Sister Harmon for a minute."

"Okay," said Nathan, heading for the door. "No problem."

Mom looked surprised. "Thanks for being so patient."

"We'll wait for you in the cultural hall," said Aria.

Mom shook her head. "I do *not* want your clothes getting dirty and torn again," she said.

"Okay," said Aria. "We'll be careful."

2

BACK TO THE TUNNEL

Aria followed Nathan out the door. They walked down the hall and into the cultural hall. It was empty, and the stage curtain was closed.

They climbed up on the stage and ducked under the curtain, heading for the costume box. "This time we're going to look like *real* pioneers," said Aria.

She pulled out a pioneer dress, apron, and bonnet. Then she hid behind a big cardboard wagon to change out of her church dress.

"Yeah, and this way Mom won't get mad about our clothes," said Nathan. He grabbed a pair of pants, a shirt, a vest, and a pioneer boy's hat. He ducked into a corner and began to change.

A few minutes later, Aria folded up her church clothes and left them in a pile. She pulled on her tennis shoes and stepped onto the stage. As Aria twirled, the pioneer dress swirled around her. She tied the faded bonnet under her chin.

"Look at me! I look just like Joseph F.," said Nathan, joining her. "Howdy, Martha Ann."

Aria giggled. "I wish we had M&M's to take to them."

"Maybe we'll get more johnnycake. Mmmm."

They jumped off the stage and opened the storage cupboard underneath. Nathan passed Aria a light to wear on her forehead.

"Perfect," said Aria. She took off the bonnet, put on the headlamp, and retied the bonnet.

The twins ducked into the cupboard. Suddenly a sizzle of electricity ran across the ground. *Zing!*

"Did you feel that?" asked Nathan.

"Yes," said Aria. "Let's go!"

They crawled forward. At first the concrete was smooth under their hands and knees. But after crawling for a few moments, they felt the ground become rocky.

"Crawling is harder in a long dress," said Aria.

"I see light ahead," said Nathan. "We're almost there!" They were in a cave now, and a small circle of light shimmered ahead.

"Do you think we'll find Joseph F. right away?" asked Nathan.

"I don't know," said Aria, crawling forward. "But that doesn't look like Little Mountain."

Nathan's head shot up. Outside the cave's entrance he could see palm trees and the sun glinting off a huge, lazy river. *Palm trees?*

"Where are we?"

3

WHERE IS GOSHEN?

Nathan and Aria stood up in the cave and crept to the entrance. The land around them was flat and green. Palm trees grew beside an enormous river that split into several smaller rivers far off in the distance. Fields and a village of houses with flat roofs shimmered in the sun.

"It's so hot!" said Nathan.

Aria nodded and tugged on her dress. The air was steamy.

"Hey! They aren't wearing pioneer clothes," said Nathan.

Coming up the path were two children. The girl was the same height as Aria. She wore a long, loose dress. Her hair was tied back, and she had a pot balanced on her head. The boy looked much younger, maybe only five years old. He wore hardly anything at all. He had a cloth around his waist and carried a small basket. They both wore leather sandals.

"Nathan, maybe you should get out the GPS and see if you can figure out where we are," said Aria, nudging him.

The children were waving at them now. "Shalom!" said the little boy.

"Shalom aleichem," said the girl.

Nathan looked at Aria in surprise. *Where are we?* he wondered.

"Ma shlomech?" asked the girl. She looked confused, as if she were wondering why Nathan and Aria were being so rude.

"Um . . . ," said Aria. "We don't understand." She looked helplessly at Nathan.

Nathan pulled his GPS out of his pocket. They had to figure out what was going on. He

pressed the power button and waited for it to load.

"Ha am otcha holech la river?" asked the girl.

"River?" said Aria. "Yes, yes, river!"

"Are you going to the river?" said the girl. Nathan looked at the GPS. It was on now. He looked from the GPS to the girl and back again.

"Oh, you speak English," said Aria. "That's great."

"English?" said the girl. "What is 'English'?" She looked at her little brother. He laughed.

"Never mind," said Aria. "What did you say about the river?"

"We are going to fetch water and herbs," said the girl. "The sun is going down. Tonight you must not be outside after dark."

Aria looked at Nathan. Were these kids crazy?

Nathan shrugged.

"Uh, right," said Aria. "We'll go to the river too, then."

"Great," said the girl. "I am Rachel, and this is Eli." They both had dark brown hair and beautiful brown eyes. Rachel's hair hung nearly to her waist. Their skin was dark from the sun.

"I have never seen clothes like yours before," said Rachel. "Or hair so bright." She reached out a hand and touched Aria's light brown hair.

Aria felt ridiculous in her pioneer bonnet and apron. And the long sleeves of the pioneer dress were horribly scratchy in the heat.

"We are visiting," Aria said.

The girl turned down the path to the river and the boy followed.

"Come on!" Eli called. He danced eagerly on the trail.

Aria waited for Nathan. "That was *so* weird,"

she said. "Why could we suddenly understand them?"

Nathan pointed to his GPS. "It happened right when I turned the GPS on. Do you think it helps us understand?"

"Maybe," whispered Aria. "Did you figure out where we are?"

Nathan held up the screen so she could see. "Goshen, Egypt," the map was labeled.

"We're in *Egypt?*" said Aria. She looked more closely at the map. "That river is the Nile!"

"I don't think they're going to have any johnnycake here," said Nathan sadly.

Aria smiled. "I have a feeling you're right about that."

"What should we do?" asked Nathan.

"Do?" said Aria. "We should see Egypt!"

"But . . . ," said Nathan. He couldn't help wondering if they should go back through the tunnel and try again. "I wanted to see Joseph F." He looked around. "I guess Egypt might be interesting. But if this is Egypt, where are the pyramids?"

4

ALONG THE RIVER

Aria and Nathan followed their new friends down to the wide, flat river. Palm trees and reeds grew along the bank. Women sat on rocks by the shallow water, scrubbing clothes in the river. Laughing and talking while they worked, the women called greetings to the children. A few stared at Nathan's and Aria's clothes.

"So much for fitting in," whispered Aria.

Eli smiled at Nathan and Aria. "I like to be a frog at the river," he said. "Ribbit, ribbit." He tried out a few froggy jumps.

"Don't let an Egyptian see you," said Rachel. "They don't like frogs right now."

"Why not?" asked Nathan. He loved frogs.

Rachel looked surprised. She carefully lifted the jug from her head and set it by the bank of the river. "Have you not heard? Last week frogs covered Egypt—you couldn't walk across the floor without squishing a dozen."

"Ugh," said Aria. She liked frogs fine, but she didn't think she would like them all over her bedroom.

"Did you keep any of the frogs for a pet?" asked Nathan.

"There were no frogs in our home," said Rachel. "But there are piles of dead frogs next to the palace. They smell so awful that no one goes near."

"Yuck," said Nathan.

"No," said Eli. "No frogs for us." He looked kind of sad about that.

The river water was silver and smooth like a long, wide ribbon. Nathan bent his legs.

"Here's a frog for you, Eli." He did a froggy jump. "Ribbit!" he called.

Eli grinned and jumped around Nathan.

Rachel pulled her dress up to her knees and waded into the water.

Aria slipped off her shoes and followed. The mud felt soft and squishy between her toes. The water moved slowly, and it was dark and cool. It felt wonderful against her hot feet and legs.

"Can I help you?" Aria asked.

Rachel showed Aria how to dip the jug into the river and fill it. The jug was heavy! Aria was afraid she might slip, but Rachel helped her lift the jug and carry it back to the bank.

"Mmmm, fresh water again," said Rachel.

"Don't you always have fresh water?" asked Aria.

Rachel's brown eyes widened with surprise. "Only a few weeks ago the Nile was red with

blood. Haven't you heard? All Egypt speaks of the plagues."

Aria choked. Suddenly she knew exactly where they were! Piles of frogs, a river of blood, and Egypt. It all made sense.

Rachel brushed back her long brown hair and looked at the sky. The sun was sinking to the edge of the sky. It looked like it would sink right into the river. "It will be getting dark. Where are you sleeping?"

Aria shook her head. "I don't know."

"You can stay with us," said Rachel.

"Yay!" said Eli. "Stay with us, stay with us."

"Tonight is the final plague. You must sleep in an Israelite home. It could mean death if you don't." Rachel's brown eyes looked serious.

"*What?*" said Nathan. This conversation wasn't making any sense to him.

Aria gave Nathan a sharp look. "I think Rachel means that the last plague will come tonight. Tomorrow *Moses* will lead the children of Israel out of Egypt."

Rachel nodded. "That's what our brother, Caleb, says."

"Ooh," said Nathan. His eyes lighted up. "I get it." He scratched his head. "We'd better go, Aria."

"Just a minute," Aria said to Rachel and Eli. They looked at her curiously as she turned back to her brother. Nathan pulled her just out of hearing.

"Let's go back to the tunnel," said Nathan. "I've heard the story of Moses. A lot of people get sick and die and stuff. Let's go home."

"But think about it," said Aria. "We would get to see Moses lead the children of Israel out of Egypt! Let's stay—just for tonight. Tomorrow morning we'll go back through the tunnel."

Nathan didn't look convinced. "I don't know," he said.

"Besides," said Aria, "tonight will be the Passover feast, and you wouldn't want to miss a big, fancy dinner." She grinned.

"Oh, fine," said Nathan. "As long as we leave first thing in the morning."

"Sure," said Aria. They walked back to Eli and Rachel. "We're coming," she said.

"Good," said Rachel. "We have to hurry. We still have to fill Eli's basket with bitter herbs."

"Bitter herbs?" mouthed Nathan. That didn't sound so promising.

Aria rolled her eyes.

5

PAINT ON THE DOOR

Rachel picked up the water jug and set it on her head. Aria didn't think that looked like a very comfortable way to carry water, but Rachel didn't seem to mind. They hurried back toward the village.

On the way they passed the entrance to the cave. Aria untied her apron and rolled it up.

Whew! She felt a little better. Aria had never been so hot in her life. She thought about taking off the bonnet, too, but decided to keep it on.

Nathan noticed what she was doing and pulled off his pioneer vest. Aria stashed the vest and apron under a bush beside the entrance to the cave.

Next to the village was a large field. Rachel and Eli led them through rows of vegetables. Rachel looked carefully at the plants.

"Grasshoppers ate the Egyptian crops," said Rachel. "So sometimes the Egyptians take ours."

"That's not fair," said Nathan.

Rachel shrugged and then knelt down by a patch of round, green stalks.

"What are they?" asked Aria, poking the plants.

"Leeks," said Rachel. She showed them how to pick the leeks by twisting them out of the ground.

Nathan grabbed one and pulled. Juice from the leek squirted onto his hand. He sniffed it. "Yuck," he said. "Smells like onions."

"Hurry!" said Rachel. "The sun is setting."

They picked as quickly as they could, stuffing leeks into the basket. When they were finished, Rachel poured a little water onto their hands to wash them.

"My fingers still smell," Nathan grumbled.

Rachel looked at the sky. "Let's go," she said. She settled the jug back on her head.

Nathan handed his scripture bag to Aria and helped Eli carry the basket.

The air was turning hazy and gray. Long black shadows in the shape of palm trees lay across the ground.

They hurried toward the village. Aria noticed that the houses had flat roofs supported by walls made of mud. People darted in and out of homes, carrying pitchers, baskets, and bundles.

"Hello, Auntie," called Rachel to a woman whose hair was covered with a brown scarf.

The woman waved. "Get inside, Rachel and Eli. This is not a night to be late."

Rachel led them down another street and

stopped in front of a home. A young man was standing in the doorway with a bowl. "Eli, Rachel, thank the Lord you are here."

"Yes, Caleb," said Rachel. "We brought the bitter herbs and water. And friends to spend the night with us."

She motioned to Aria and Nathan.

"Welcome," said Caleb. "This night you must not be alone. Come and help me mark the door."

Rachel and Eli put the water and herbs in the house.

Aria smiled shyly at Caleb. He was an older teenage boy. His skin was brown from the sun, and his eyes were kind.

"Would you like to see?" He held out the bowl. It looked like it was filled with bright red paint. He picked up a brush made from branches.

"Now," said Caleb, "we mark our door with lamb's blood."

"Lamb's blood?" said Nathan. "Ugh." He hadn't remembered that part of the story.

Caleb dipped the brush into the blood. He painted a long stroke down one side of the door. "Anyone else want to try?"

"I do," said Aria. She dipped the brush, and Caleb lifted her up to paint a stroke down the other side. The blood was bright red, and a little got on Aria's hand. She rubbed it off with her other hand.

"Anyone else?" asked Caleb.

"No, thanks," said Nathan.

Caleb painted one final stroke across the top. Smeared around the door, the blood looked pretty scary.

Aria looked down the street. Other people were doing the same thing to their doors. "This blood means we know the God of Abraham," said Caleb. "The plague will pass over our house."

Aria felt a prickle of fear in her heart. Would they be safe?

6

THE DARK NIGHT

"Come on," said Eli, darting through the door.

Nathan and Aria entered the house. Inside they found a small table, jars of herbs, and bundles leaning against the wall. On one side of the room a woman stood in front of a fire, slowing turning a sizzling piece of meat.

"Ima!" said Eli. "We brought friends."

Eli's mother smiled at Nathan and Aria. "Welcome," she said. Her eyes were brown and kind like Rachel's. Her skin was wrinkled and dry, as if she had spent many days working outside. "Tonight we are having a special meal," she said.

"We can help," said Aria. Soon she was

busy helping Rachel chop leeks. Nathan and Eli set the table with pottery. Auntie arrived with her husband and three little children, so the small house was soon bursting with people and smells and sounds. Outside the night had grown very dark.

They gathered around the table, and Caleb said a prayer. "Blessed art Thou, O Lord our God," he said. Then the food was passed. Nathan loaded his plate with roast lamb, a flat piece of soft bread, and steamed vegetables. He took one leek just to be polite, but he hoped no one would notice that he didn't eat it.

Before Nathan could start eating, Caleb spoke. "For four hundred years our people have been slaves in Egypt. We have had to work in the hot sun, making bricks for a pharaoh who does not believe in our God. But the Lord has heard our prayers and sent the prophet Moses to deliver us."

"Why are we eating bitter herbs tonight?" asked Eli.

Caleb smiled. "Tonight we eat the bitter herbs to remember how bitter slavery has been. But tomorrow we will be free."

Nathan squirmed in his seat. He thought that if Eli and his family could be slaves, he could probably eat a leek. He crunched on one end. It was hot and spicy and made tears spring to his eyes. "Yuck," he whispered to Aria. "The leek tastes awful."

"I think it's supposed to taste awful," said Aria. "It tastes like being a slave feels." She smiled. "Try the bread. It's not johnnycake, but it's delicious."

Nathan broke off a piece. It was warm and soft. Mmmm. And the roast lamb reminded him of the steak his mom sometimes cooked for a special meal. He was glad they had stayed.

After dinner, Caleb and Ima sang beautiful

songs. The words sounded like they might be scriptures.

The songs made Aria sleepy. She yawned. The fire had died down, and the room was very dark. A small oil lamp was the only light. She was ready for bed. She looked around the small room and wondered where they would all sleep. Ima and Caleb pushed the table to one side of the room and spread mats upon the floor. They gave Aria a blanket, but the air was still so hot she didn't think she would need it.

Nathan and Aria lay down in one corner. Rachel and Eli stretched out nearby. Aria could see into the black night sky through a little square window. A full moon hung there, pale and yellow.

Nathan drifted off to sleep quickly. But Aria noticed that the adults did not lie down. They kept their shoes on, and Caleb had his staff in his hand. They seemed to be waiting for

something. Then Aria was too tired to think about it anymore.

She was sound asleep when she heard an awful scream.

"What was that?" Nathan asked, sitting up-right.

The house was completely dark, but they heard feet running outside.

Another scream came and then crying. Aria reached for Nathan, and they held onto each other. Caleb's voice came to them through the darkness. "It's okay," he said. "The Egyptians are suffering because their king's heart is hard. But we are safe."

It was difficult to sleep with people crying in the dark. Aria wrapped the blanket around herself and tried not to miss her mother. It seemed the night would never end.

7

A CLOUD BY DAY

When the sky was barely light, Ima arose and began mixing bread. Aria helped her stir the dough, but they had only stirred a few times when a sharp knock came at the door.

A voice outside said, "Time to go. Pharaoh has set us free!"

Up and down the street the message passed. "We can leave. We are free."

"Come," said Caleb. "Gather your things. Today we follow Moses out of Egypt."

Then it seemed that everyone was running, packing, and tying things into bundles.

Auntie and Uncle left for their own house. "See you in the caravan," they said.

Ima put the bread dough on the kneading

trough. "It has no time to rise," she said. "Perhaps the sun will bake it as we walk."

Caleb brought a donkey with baskets strapped to its back. Nathan wondered if the donkey would really be able to carry so much through the desert. "Poor donkey," he said, patting its scratchy fur.

"Hee-haw," said the donkey.

The streets were a mad rush of people and animals. People carried babies, geese, blankets, and baskets of figs. They rushed in every direction.

"There are so many people!" said Aria.

"Come," said Caleb. "It's time to go."

"I want to walk with Auntie," said Eli.

"Okay," said Ima. "Go with them, but meet us for supper."

Eli skipped down the street to Auntie's house.

Nathan grabbed his scripture bag and

followed Caleb through the crowded streets. They joined the stream of people gathering on a huge plain. There were people and animals in every direction as far as Aria could see.

"Look at the camels!" said Nathan. Their silly expressions made him laugh.

Far away, at the front of the group, Aria saw a man with white hair holding a staff. *Is that Moses?* she wondered.

The sky was blue except for one white fluffy cloud above the front of the caravan. The cloud moved forward, and someone blew a horn. All the animals and people began walking, and the air grew thick with dust.

"Look!" said Aria, nudging Nathan. "Do you see that cloud?"

Nathan nodded.

"I think that's the cloud that tells them where to go. The scriptures say they followed a cloud by day and a pillar of fire by night."

"Wow," said Nathan. "That's even better than a GPS."

Aria laughed.

"Good-bye!" called Rachel.

"Thank you!" said Nathan and Aria. They waved until the caravan was out of sight.

"I wish we could go with them and see Moses part the sea," said Aria.

"Yeah, but I wouldn't want to be there when Pharaoh shows up," said Nathan.

Then the twins sat down and ate the small breakfast Ima had made for them. Nathan ate some leftover bread while Aria munched on figs and white cheese. When they were finished, they stood up and brushed the crumbs off their clothes.

"Now, let's get back to the tunnel before the trouble starts," said Nathan.

"Good idea," said Aria.

They turned and walked back through

the village. It was silent now. All the homes were quiet. The streets were empty except for things people had dropped—a squished melon, a piece of cloth, a ring. Aria bent over and picked up the ring. It was gold with a blue carved stone in the center.

"I wonder who dropped it," said Aria.

"Good luck finding them," said Nathan.

Aria slipped the ring on her finger, wondering what to do with it. It fit perfectly, but she didn't want to take something that didn't belong to her.

They passed Rachel's house.

"What's that sound?" asked Aria.

"What?" asked Nathan.

"I hear crying." Aria pushed open the door to Rachel's house. Inside they found Eli, curled up under the table, sobbing.

8

RUN FOR THE SEA

"Eli!" said Nathan. "What are you doing here?"

"I went to Auntie's house, but they had left already. Then I came back here, but everyone was gone. I want Ima!" he cried.

Aria looked at Nathan in alarm.

"We can't follow them," said Nathan. "Pharaoh's army is coming."

Aria nodded. "And if we cross the Red Sea, we won't be able to get back to the tunnel." She looked down at the little boy. "But what about Eli?"

"We can't just leave him," said Nathan.

Aria tried to listen to her heart. What was the right thing to do? Her mother would be worried sick if they couldn't get home. And they didn't want to be Israelites forever! But she also knew they had to help Eli. "Help us do the right thing, Heavenly Father," she prayed silently. She felt peaceful and calm inside.

"We're not going to leave him," Aria said.

"What are we going to do?" asked Nathan.

"We're going to take him to his family!" said Aria. "I don't know how the enchanted tunnel works, but I feel that it's going to be okay somehow."

"All right," said Nathan. "I hope so. But we're going to have to go fast! Come on, Eli." Nathan handed Aria his scripture bag and lifted the little boy onto his shoulders for a piggyback ride. "Let's watch Pharaoh get creamed!"

Eli hung onto Nathan, and they rushed back through the empty streets.

"Whee!" said Nathan, trying to make Eli laugh. They ran back to the gathering place.

"They're gone," said Eli. He looked as if he might start crying again.

"It's okay," said Aria. "Nathan has a really good map." She helped Eli down from Nathan's back so Nathan could pull out the GPS.

"The Red Sea is that way," said Nathan, pointing. "Let's go!"

As they walked into the desert, the green land disappeared. After they passed the last palm tree, ahead they saw only rocks, sand, and more rocks. The sun was so hot that Aria guessed it would cook Ima's bread dough in just a few minutes.

"We're going to get sunburned!" said Aria. She was glad now that she had the bonnet.

"Good thing I brought water," said Nathan. He pulled the bottle out of his scripture bag and gave Eli a drink.

It was hard to hurry in the heat of the day.

"I think being a pioneer was easy compared to being an Israelite," said Nathan.

Aria looked down at her dusty shoes. "They had a lot in common," she said. At least she had worn sneakers this time.

After an hour or so, Eli said, "I can't walk anymore."

Nathan looked at the GPS. "We're almost there, Eli. You can do it. How about one more piggyback ride?"

Eli climbed up, and Nathan took off at a gallop. The road was getting steeper and wound up a large hill. From the top, they could see a sparkle of water in the distance.

"Look!" said Aria. "The Red Sea!" An enormous crowd of people and animals had gathered near its shore. "Your family is down there, Eli."

"Yay!" said Eli. "We found them."

"Uh-oh," said Nathan. "Do you feel that?"

The ground rumbled. Behind them, dust clouds filled the air.

"It's Pharaoh's army," said Aria. "We have to get out of here!"

Eli whimpered. "Ima, Ima."

Nathan picked up Eli, and the kids ran for their lives. Aria had never run so fast before. Soon her chest was burning, but she knew they couldn't stop. Her feet pounded the dirt, and dust choked her throat. She could hear Nathan behind her. The rumbling was getting louder.

The road dipped down to the sea. Aria could see the Israelites pointing to the road behind her, shouting.

Suddenly, Aria's foot caught on a rock. She tripped and fell.

Nathan stopped, and Eli jumped to the ground.

"Aria, are you all right?" cried Nathan. He pulled on her arm. "You have to get up!"

Aria tried to get up, but her feet wouldn't move.

Just then, the army came over the top of the hill.

Aria and Nathan could see horses and chariots and Egyptian soldiers with spears. Their armor flashed in the sun. The chariots were decorated with blue, red, and gold. The soldiers rushed toward them in a blur of galloping horses and dust.

9

A PATH IN THE DEEP

"Come on, Aria!" Nathan begged.

Aria stared at the army. She tried to scramble to her feet as the soldiers marched closer and closer.

Suddenly there was a flash of light. Frightened horses neighed. The chariots pulled up short and stopped in a haze of dust. A thick cloud suddenly blocked their way.

Nathan reached for his sister. "Are you okay?" he asked again.

Aria nodded. Nathan helped her stand up.

Eli was crying. He wrapped his arms around Aria. "I thought the horses would smoosh you," he said.

Aria laughed. "Me too!" She rubbed her

ankle. It was a little sore, and her hands were scratched. She glanced back at the army. They were pointing at the cloud that had stopped them, trying to figure out what it was.

"Let's take you to your family," Aria said to Eli. She picked up Nathan's scripture bag.

They turned toward the Red Sea. The people were gathered next to the water. In front, the man with white hair was standing on a rock. He held a staff in his hands. Suddenly he reached his arms out over the water. A gust of wind swept from the man across the water. And then, the water began to *move*.

"Look!" said Nathan.

"What is it?" said Eli.

"Your family is trapped," said Aria. "So Moses is making a way out."

"Through the *sea*?" said Eli.

"Do you have a better idea?" Nathan asked, teasing.

Eli shook his head. His mouth hung open.

The water was white and frothy like the ocean in a storm. Then it looked as if someone had unzipped an enormous zipper in the middle of the water. The sound was like a flood. Swwwwiiiissssshhhhhh.

A path appeared in the middle of the sea, with walls of water on either side. Moses stepped onto the path and walked into the sea on dry ground. The people slowly followed him, looking scared, amazed, and hopeful all at once.

Nathan, Aria, and Eli caught up with the last few people just as they were stepping onto the path.

The last people were the slowest travelers: old men and women and mothers carrying babies. Some looked sick, and one man had a bandaged leg.

"Come, Mother," said another man. He was leading a woman whose hair was pure white.

"Will the water stay back?" the woman asked. She pointed to the walls of water, her finger trembling.

"The prophet is leading us," said the man. "He knows the way."

Aria and Nathan looked up at the huge walls of water reaching to the sky. The water was white and frothing.

"I don't want to go," said Eli.

"It's going to be okay," said Aria. "I promise."

"How can you be sure?" said Eli, his lips pouting.

Aria smiled at Nathan.

"Trust me, she knows," said Nathan.

"Okay," said Eli.

They stepped onto the path and walked into the middle of the sea. The ground felt

sandy and a little slimy. Their feet crunched on rocks and seaweed. The sea floor dipped down.

"I'm cold!" said Eli. A strong, wet wind was blowing. Soon they were soaking wet.

Nathan looked up at the walls of water. They stretched so high that he could see only a little bit of sky at the very top. "Look, Eli. A fish!" The fish leaped out for a moment and then was lost in the frothy white.

Soon they saw beautiful pink corals. Aria thought they looked like flowers made out of rock. They walked for a long time. Then the ground began to tilt upwards.

Nathan glanced behind him. "Look out," he said, "here come the chariots!"

Aria looked back too. The chariot wheels turned slowly in the sand, but the army was catching up. "Hurry!" she cried.

They rushed for the bank, climbing up

and up. The old woman and her son rushed too. Some people were screaming. Then, just before they reached the bank, they heard the loudest crash they had ever heard in their life. It sounded like a tall building breaking apart. They felt a gust of wind, followed by the sound of smashing water.

"The sea is closing," cried Nathan. "Come on!" He carried Eli, pushing him up on the bank.

Aria was last. She threw the scripture bag onto the bank and felt water wash around her feet and up to her knees. "Help!" she cried.

A strong hand caught her arm and pulled her up. "There you go, little one," said a voice.

Aria looked up. A man with white, flowing hair and kind, brown eyes smiled down at her. He wore a red robe and held a wooden staff in his hands. "You are very brave, my child," he said. "We would not wish to leave you with the Egyptians."

"Thank you," said Aria. She looked up at his face. His eyes were full of light. She knew exactly who he was. "Thank you very much."

10

MIRIAM'S SONG

"Wow," said Nathan when he saw who had helped Aria.

Moses smiled kindly at them both and then turned and disappeared into the crowd.

Aria stared at her hand.

"Look!" said Nathan, pointing to the water.

Aria turned. Egyptian shields floated on the waves, bobbing up and down.

"Hey," said Eli. He looked from Aria to Nathan. "How did you know everything would be okay?"

Nathan shrugged. "Lucky guess?"

Aria grinned.

They turned away from the sea and walked into the crowd of people. Some were weeping, others were laughing, and many were praying. They looked as if they couldn't believe what had just happened. Aria noticed that the only cloud in the sky was right above them.

"We are free!" said the old woman to her son. Tears streamed down her face. He held her and nodded.

"Eli!" called Ima. "Eli! We were so worried."

Eli ran straight into his mother's arms. Caleb and Rachel and Auntie and Uncle all tried to hug him at once.

Eli pointed to Nathan and Aria. Eli's family turned and pulled Nathan and Aria into the circle too. It was a big circle of hugging and laughing and crying.

"And then Moses saved Aria," said Eli. "And we were all safe."

Caleb smiled, hugging Eli as if he would never let go. "Yes, we are safe. And we are going to follow the prophet to the promised land, a place where there will be milk and honey."

Aria remembered the ring she had found. She slipped it off her finger and held it up to Caleb. "We found this in the street when we went back. Do you know who it belongs to?"

Caleb looked at the stone. "It's an Egyptian scarab ring. Many Egyptians wanted us to leave. They gave us their jewelry and begged us to go." He looked at Aria. "You have been very brave and honest as well. Keep the ring."

Aria smiled and slipped the ring back on her finger.

Suddenly the air was filled with music. Aria heard the tinkling of instruments. A beautiful woman with a long blue scarf and twisting brown curls shook a tambourine and sang in a voice that was sweet and strong.

"Hashira la adonai," she sang. "Sing to the

Lord, for He is mighty," she continued. It was a lovely, haunting song.

Ima smiled. "Miriam the prophetess is singing her praise."

Other women took up their tambourines and joined Miriam. Dancing in circles with pure joy upon their faces, they praised God for His miraculous deliverance.

Rachel took Aria's hand. "Come on," she said. "Let's join them."

Aria held back for a moment, but then she let the music lead her feet. She lifted her arms and danced across the sand with the other women, singing and praising the Lord. The song filled her heart. She had never felt so happy.

The celebration lasted all afternoon. When the sun dipped low in the sky, Nathan finally said, "We'd better go."

Aria nodded.

"Where are you going?" asked Eli.

"Will you be all right?" asked Rachel.

Aria bit her lip. She *hoped* they would be.

"We'll be okay," said Nathan.

"Good-bye!" said Rachel.

Eli hugged Aria. "Thank you for helping me. I'm so glad you didn't get smooshed."

Aria laughed. "Me too, Eli."

"'Bye!" Nathan waved.

They walked through the crowd. People were setting up camp for the night. They heard people speaking of the promised land.

"I would hate to tell them they're not going to get there for a while," said Aria. "Forty years is a long time."

Nathan laughed. "Just let them be happy tonight."

11

THE ENCHANTED TUNNEL

Finally Aria and Nathan made it through the crowd and turned toward the desert. "Now where?" asked Nathan.

"I don't know," said Aria. "I hoped you had an idea."

"Nope," said Nathan. "But I figured that if God could part the Red Sea to save Rachel and Eli, He would help us get home again, too."

"I agree," said Aria. "Remember what Joseph F. did? Let's say a prayer."

Nathan said a prayer, asking for help.

Aria felt peaceful and calm. She knew that everything would be okay somehow.

"I have an idea," said Nathan. "Let's check the GPS for caves around here."

"Good idea," said Aria.

Nathan pulled it out. "It says there are some caves that way. Do you think the tunnel followed us?"

"I really hope so," said Aria, "because it is a long way back through the Red Sea."

Nathan and Aria ran toward the hills. The ground looked shadowy and gray. They climbed around the edges of the hills, looking for openings, but it was hard to see because it was almost dark. The hills seemed to be made of piles of rocks and more rocks.

At last they saw a small crack in a hillside. "That could be a cave," said Aria.

Nathan pulled the headlamps out of his scripture bag.

"I hope these still work," he said, handing one to Aria. He clicked his on.

"Mine works, too," said Aria.

"Let's check out the cave," said Nathan. He

walked into the opening, and Aria followed. It was pitch black and bigger than it looked from the outside. They followed the passage, which twisted and turned.

"I really hope a bear doesn't live in here," said Aria. "Or a bat." She gulped. Her skin felt all shivery in the darkness. She kept checking behind them.

"Look!" said Nathan. "A tunnel."

"But is it the *right* tunnel?" asked Aria.

"There's only one way to find out!" Nathan knelt down and crawled into the tunnel. Aria knelt down too.

A sizzle of electricity ran along the ground.

"I think this is it," said Nathan. They crawled for several moments, and soon the ground felt smooth and cold under their hands.

"A square of light!" said Aria. It was the

cupboard door. Nathan pushed it open and helped Aria to her feet.

They were standing in the cultural hall. "We made it!" said Nathan.

Aria started to cry. "I wasn't sure we would."

"Yes, you were," said Nathan. "You said it was going to be okay. And it was."

Aria smiled and wiped her tears away. "Well, I was a little worried."

A door opened, and they saw their mom's curly red hair through the doorway. "Are you two ready?"

Her mouth dropped when she saw their clothes. "Are those church costumes?" She looked really mad. She walked closer and touched Aria's dress. "They're filthy! You two are in big trouble."

Aria threw her arms around her mom and hugged her as tight as she could. "I love you!" she said.

Mom looked surprised but hugged her back. She sighed. "I love you too, Aria. Ready to go home?"

"Yes!" said Nathan and Aria at the same time.

12

ALL THE PIECES

"I'll meet you at the computer!" said Nathan as he walked by Aria's door.

"I'm coming," said Aria. "Wait for me."

Aria and Nathan stopped by their mom's room.

"Is it okay if we use the computer?" Aria asked.

"For a few minutes," said Mom.

Aria's hair was wet from her bath. Her nightgown felt warm and soft. At dinner she'd drunk so much water that Mom had said, "You're drinking as if you'd just walked across a desert."

Nathan had laughed and laughed.

Aria and Nathan sat down in front of the computer together. Aria opened an Internet window and typed in "Moses." She clicked on an article and read:

"After the children of Israel crossed the Red Sea, Moses led them to Mount Sinai, where he received the Ten Commandments written on stone tablets by the hand of God. He led them through the wilderness for forty years, where they saw many miracles. When they arrived at the border of the land of Israel, Moses sent twelve spies into the land. Only Joshua and Caleb brought back a good report."

"Wow," said Nathan. "Rachel and Eli probably saw Moses come down with the Ten Commandments. That's so cool."

Aria smiled. "I hope they made it to the promised land." She looked at the article again. "Wait a minute. Do you think that could be the Caleb *we* met?"

"Maybe," said Nathan. "Is he in the scriptures?"

"Yes," said Aria. "In the Old Testament."

"Then I guess they made it through the desert."

"And I helped Caleb mark his door for Passover!" said Aria.

Nathan leaned back on his stool, balancing on the back legs. "Now we know that the tunnel doesn't always take us to the same place every time."

Aria nodded. "I wonder what makes it decide where to take us?" She held out her hand to admire the blue scarab ring.

Nathan pointed to their pioneer costumes sitting in a basket in the corner. "Mom was really mad about the church costumes. And we lost the vest and apron. We're going to have to figure out something else to wear if we go back."

"*When* we go back," said Aria.

They both smiled.

EPILOGUE

The story of Moses leading the children of Israel out of Egypt is spoken of often in the scriptures. Shortly before Moses was born, Pharaoh commanded that all Hebrew male babies be killed. To save her son, Moses' mother made a basket out of reeds and put him in the river.

Moses' older sister, Miriam, watched to see what would happen to him. Pharaoh's daughter saw the basket and had it pulled from the river. When she saw the baby inside, she decided to raise him as her own.

When Moses grew up, one day he saw an Egyptian beating a Hebrew slave. Moses tried to stop the beating and killed the Egyptian.

Afraid of Pharaoh, he fled into the wilderness, where he became a shepherd and married a shepherd girl.

One day when Moses was leading his flocks, he saw a bush that was on fire but did not burn up. He went to look at the bush, and the Lord spoke to him, commanding him to return to Egypt and free the children of Israel.

Pharaoh refused to let the slaves go free, so the Lord sent plagues to soften his heart. The plagues of locusts, hail, frogs, and flies destroyed the crops and flocks in Egypt, but the Israelite lands were spared. Still Pharaoh refused to let them go.

Even after five more plagues, Pharaoh's heart still had not softened. The Lord commanded Moses that each Israelite family should kill a pure white lamb and paint the blood on the top and sides of the door. Every family ate a special meal of lamb meat, unleavened bread, and bitter herbs. They ate the meal dressed for a journey, with shoes on their feet and a staff in their hand. That night, the final plague passed through the land. The firstborn child in every home died except in the homes marked with blood. The plague *passed over* those homes.

Finally, Pharaoh let the children of Israel leave. They traveled to the Red Sea, camping in several places along the way. (The time and distance of the Israelites' journey are compressed in *Escape from Egypt*.)

But Pharaoh changed his mind and chased after them with his chariots. They were trapped between the army and the sea, but God sent an angel and a cloud to stop the army. Then Moses raised his staff and stretched his hand over the sea and divided it. The children of Israel walked through on dry ground. They were free at last.

The Lord commanded the children of Israel

to celebrate the Passover forever (Exodus 12:14). It was celebrated throughout Old Testament times and is still celebrated by observant Jews today.

Latter-day Saints believe that the Passover lamb was a symbol of the Savior. Jesus celebrated the Passover with his disciples. In fact, the Last Supper was a Passover meal. At that meal, Jesus used the Passover bread and wine to begin the sacrament. Today when we take the sacrament, we remember the Savior as the Lamb of God whose blood was shed so that spiritual death will pass over us.

Caleb was one of twelve spies sent into the land of Israel to see if the children of Israel should enter the land. Ten of the spies said the Israelites would be defeated by the people who already lived there.

But Joshua and Caleb said the Israelites should trust the Lord to deliver them. Because of his faith, Caleb was blessed to enter Israel and receive an inheritance. The Lord said Caleb "followed me fully" (Numbers 14:24).

FUN FACTS

The Hebrew word for "mother" is *Ima*. "Father" is *Abba*.

The Pharaoh of Moses' day was probably Ramses II. He was called Ramses the Great and built more temples than any other Pharaoh. The children of Israel lived in Goshen and probably worked to build the palaces, temples, and statues of Pharaoh. The pyramids are not near Goshen and were built hundreds of years earlier.

Carvings of scarabs were very popular in Egyptian jewelry. The scarab was a beetle, which represented life. Scarab jewelry was often believed to have special protective powers. When the children of Israel left, the Egyptians gave them jewelry and begged them to leave before Egypt was destroyed.

During their time of slavery, the children of Israel were forced to make bricks from mud and straw. The mud and straw were put into a pit. Then the people mixed them together with their feet by tramping the straw into the mud. This was very hard work! When the mixture was ready, it was put into molds and set out to dry in the sun.

Tradition says the first *matzo* (unleavened bread) was made on the morning of the Exodus. The women made dough without any leavening and carried it in their kneading troughs. The desert sun baked it hard and flat as they walked.

Miriam was called a prophetess. In the Old Testament, the words *prophet* and *prophetess* are often used for a man and a woman who have the spiritual gift of prophecy, which is the "testimony of Jesus" (Revelation 19:10). Today the word *prophet* usually refers to the president of the Church, who holds all of the priesthood keys (see Daniel H. Ludlow, "I Have a Question," *Ensign,* December 1980, 31–32).

After the miracle of the parting of the Red Sea, Miriam led the other women in praising the Lord in dance and song. The words to her song are recorded in Exodus 15:20–21.

TO LEARN MORE

You can learn more about the first Passover and the departure of the children of Israel from Egypt by reading these books yourself or by asking a parent or teacher to help you:

The book of Exodus in the Old Testament, especially chapters 2 through 15.

Celebrating Passover: A Guide to Understanding the Jewish Feast for Latter-day Saints, by Marianne Monson-Burton (Bountiful, Utah: Horizon Publishers, 2004).

My First Passover Board Book (New York: DK Publishing, 2002).

Exodus, by Brian Wildsmith (Grand Rapids, Mich.: Eerdmans, 1998).

THE MATZO-MAKING SONG

Many songs are sung during the Passover. Most are hymns or words of scripture set to music. Others are fun songs for children. This song is about making matzo, or unleavened bread, and is sung to the tune of "Row, Row, Row Your Boat":

Roll, roll, roll your dough
  (rub palms together in circular motion),
Make it nice and round
  (pretend to form a ball),
Make it flat *(slap hands together)*,
Poke lots of holes
  (pretend to poke holes in hand),
And bake it 'til it's brown
  (pretend to put it in the oven).

ABOUT THE AUTHOR

Marianne Monson spent much of her childhood looking for magic passageways. Reading good books has always been one of her favorite adventures. She studied English at Brigham Young University and also spent a semester in Jerusalem, where she crawled through Hezekiah's Tunnel. Now she particularly enjoys following her children, Nathan and Aria, as they discover their own enchanted tunnels.

Marianne holds an MFA from Vermont College in writing for children and young adults. She teaches creative writing at Portland Community College and serves as a Gospel Doctrine teacher in her ward in Hillsboro, Oregon. You can visit her at www.MarianneMonson.com.